Boing—Boing

THE BIONIC CAT

Boing-Boing

THE BIONIC CAT

Written by Larry L. Hench
Illustrations by Ruth Denise Lear

Published by The Can of Worms Kids Press

1 3 5 7 9 10 8 6 4 2

First published in the UK in 2004 by
Can of Worms Kids Press
2 Peacock Yard
London SE17 3LH
United Kingdom

Telephone: +44 (0)845 123 3971
E-mail: info@canofwormspress.co.uk
Web site: www.canofwormspress.co.uk

Copyright © Can of Worms Enterprises Ltd 2004
Text Copyright © Larry L. Hench

First published in hardback by the American Ceramic Society 2000
ISBN: 1-57498-109-9

Printed and bound in Italy
Cover design – Alison Eddy
Text design – Shona O'Connor, Robert Whitaker
Producer – Can of Worms Design Group

A CIP catalogue record for this book is available from the British
Library

ISBN: 1-904872-00-X

For Daniel, who read it first.

Professor George says...

Dear Readers

When Larry Hench became a grandfather, he started looking for books to read to his grandchildren that taught science concepts in a fun and interesting way, without talking down, through stories that were realistic—not fairytale-like. He couldn't find them; he was also dismayed to see scientists, professors, and engineers portrayed as evil, nutty, nerdy, absent-minded, etc…not as real, caring, helpful human beings. Larry wanted children to see the excitement and process of science, and scientists and engineers as trustworthy, interesting, and fun people. So he decided to write his own stories to accomplish these goals. Enter Boing-Boing!

Parents and Teachers: While these books have been written for enjoyment they have also been adopted by schools to help teach children aged seven and up about science and technology. In the Boing-Boing the Bionic Cat series the general synopsis of the books is as follows: Daniel, who loves cats but is allergic to them, is delighted when his inventive neighbour Professor George—that's me, an engineer— builds him a bionic cat with fibre-optic fur, computer-controlled joints, electronic eyes, and ceramic-sensor whiskers. It's just like a real cat, but Daniel is not allergic to it! With each succeeding adventure I add new technological features to Boing-Boing. Everything that I make Boing-Boing do in this book can be done at home or at school.

Glossary: Throughout the book you will find some words highlighted in bold. These words may be difficult for some readers to understand, so at the end of this book you will find a glossary explaining their meanings.

If you have any questions about Boing-Boing please do not hesitate to write to me by e-mail: professor.george@boing-boing.org or by post: Professor George, c/o Can of Worms Press, 2 Peacock Yard, London SE17 3LH, United Kingdom.

Contents

Bionic Cat

Bionic Eyes
(optical sensors that detect
light, dark, and motion)

Bionic Whiskers
(piezoelectric ceramics on
the end of metallic
conductors that convert
heat, pressure, and
mechanical deflection
into electrical signals)

Computer
(small, powerful,
programmable microprocessor
that converts electrical
signals from sensors to control
bionic legs, tail, head, and
voice box)

Bionic Tail
(four multi-axial joints
that enable tail to
move in all directions
under computer control

Design Features

Fibre-Optic Fur
(optical glass fibre, covering over all surfaces, that transmits sunlight through the fibres to photoelectric cells that charge the batteries)

Bionic Voice Box
(programmable voice simulator activated by sensors embedded in the fibre-optic fur; controlled by the computer)

Batteries
(6 rechargeable 9-volt batteries that provide power to the computer, the bionic eyes, tail, legs, head, and ceramic heating elements)

Bionic Legs
(4 legs with 3 multi-axial joints per leg connected to small motors controlled by the computer)

Chapter One

Daniel was sitting on the front steps of his house with his head in his hands.

He wiped away a tear that dripped down his cheek as he remembered his mother's words from a few minutes earlier.

"Daniel, I've told you for the last time you cannot have a cat! Now run outside and play and stop bothering me. I've got work to do! I have had it right up to here about cats!" she said, holding her hand up to her neck.

"But why not Mummy?" Daniel said. "I promise to take care of it. I really will. I promise. I promise," he pleaded.

His mother sighed a great big sigh. "Daniel, if I've told you once, I've told you a million times: you cannot have a cat because you are allergic to them.

"Every time you pet a cat you start sneezing and get red blotches all over you.

"The doctor says if you have a cat your allergy will only get worse."

Sitting on the steps, Daniel was sad because he knew his mother was right. "She's always right, " he grumbled.

Just then Daniel looked up and saw his neighbour, Professor George, walking up the road.

"What's the matter, Dan?" Professor George asked. "You really do look miserable."

"I am Professor George," Daniel answered. "My Mum won't let me have a cat."

"That's a shame," replied the professor. "Why not? Does she think you won't take care of it?"

"No," answered Daniel. "It's because I'm allergic to cats. They make me sneeze and break out in red spots when I pet them. I guess I'll just never have a cat," Daniel moaned.

"Well, I don't know about that," Professor George said. "Never say never. Many things change for the better with time. Just be patient, Dan," he said. "Maybe something will happen so you can have a cat someday."

Professor George had the beginning of an idea. He started whistling as he walked home, letting the idea grow in his mind with more and more detail.

By the time he got home, Professor George knew what he was going to do. He was going to build Daniel a **bionic** cat. "It will be like some of the **robots** we build in my lab," he thought. "But Dan's bionic cat must also be like a real cat. That will be a real challenge."

Professor George taught students about bioengineering, but he was no ordinary professor. He gave lectures and went to meetings, just like the other professors at the big university nearby; but he was also head of a robotics and engineering research laboratory at the university.

His laboratory was very special. He and his students did research and built robots. Their robots were not at all like the robots in the movies. They were robots used to make cars, trains and big machines.

For relaxation, Professor George liked to spend time in the workshop he had made in his basement at home. It wasn't an ordinary workshop. In it he had all sorts of tools and electronic gadgets and a **computer** connected to the big **Super Computer** at the university.

Professor George gave his wife a quick kiss when he got home, then he went straight down to his workshop. "I'm going to work on a little project, for Dan next door."

He sat down at his computer and connected it to the Super Computer. He quickly did some calculations. Then he did some design drawings on his computer. When he had finished, Professor George leaned back and stretched with a big smile on his face. He chuckled. "It looks like it can be done," he said.

Chapter Two

After a quick dinner and apologies to his wife, Professor George went back downstairs to his workshop. He started building a little robot. He worked on and

on. It got later and later.

His wife came down to the workshop and said, as she gave him a kiss good night, "George, you can stay up all night if you want to, but I am going to bed. Good night."

"Good night, sweetheart," Professor George answered. "It shouldn't take too much longer. I want to finish now that I'm this far along."

Unfortunately, he was wrong. The sun was just coming up when Professor George stretched and said to himself with a big yawn, "Oh boy, I think it's finally finished."

He got up from his workbench and rubbed his eyes. He looked down at what was sitting there looking up at him. "It really looks real," he said to himself, with a smile. "I've made a bionic cat that looks just like a real cat."

The little robot was just the size of a cat. It had four legs that could move with **battery** power, and light-yellow electronic eyes that told the little computer inside its belly where it was going.

It even had whiskers on either side of a little nose. The whiskers ended with tiny little electronic **ceramic sensors** that also were connected to the little computer inside. When the whiskers touched something they sent a signal to the little computer, telling the bionic cat to move around the object.

It had a tail that moved. But, best of all, the bionic cat had fur. Its fur was very, very special. It was **fibre-optic** fur.

The fibre-optic fur soaks up the sunshine when the bionic cat sits in the window, as cats like to do. The sunlight travels down the glass fibres to the inside of the cat where it is changed into electricity by a **solar cell**.

"Let's check out your fibre-optic fur, little fellow," said Professor George as he put a special bulb in his desk lamp. He shone the lamp onto the bionic cat.

"Now, let's see whether the light is charging your batteries," he said as he looked at the meter hooked up to the inside of the bionic cat.

"Good, it's nine volts, that's just right," Professor George said. "The electricity will keep your batteries charged. You can act just like a real cat. You can sit and catnap in the sunshine during the day. That will charge your batteries. Then, if you want to, you can run around all night."

Professor George was very pleased with his creation, in spite of being very sleepy. He had enjoyed building the bionic cat almost as much as he enjoyed teaching his engineering students.

He picked up the bionic cat and said to him as he gently stroked its fur, "Well, it does feel real – just what I was hoping

for. If you can't pet a cat, you might as well not have one."

Next, he felt under the bionic cat's belly and switched on the batteries.

"Let's see how you work, little fellow." The eyes lit up with a very pleasant soft yellow glow. The **pupils** in the eyes got smaller when a lot of light shone on them. They opened wide when there was only a little bit of light. "So far, so good," Professor George said to the bionic cat.

Next he lightly stroked the fur. The

bionic cat responded with a very pleasing "purrr, purrr, purrr," from its mouth and the small **voice simulator** located in its throat.

"That sounds just right," Professor George responded.

"Now, let's see how you get around," he said as he set the bionic cat down on the floor. Immediately the cat started walking around the cluttered workshop with its tail switching back and forth.

When the bionic cat got close to a pile of books, some of its whiskers warned it to walk around them.

When it got close to the electric heater sitting on the floor, its whiskers warned it electronically, "Too hot. Too hot," and the bionic cat backed away from the heater.

"Very good. Very, very good job, kitty," chuckled Professor George. "I think you'll work just fine, just fine indeed. I can't wait to see Daniel's face when he sees you.

"Well, I think that is everything," Professor George said to himself. "All systems seem to be working properly. I'd better rush. I have a class to teach in two hours and I need a hot shower and some breakfast to wake me up."

Chapter Three

J ust as he was leaving the workshop, Professor George remembered one more thing. "Oh no," he said. "I forgot to check to see if the bionic cat can speak."

So, he picked up the cat and switched on its batteries. He rubbed the bionic cat's nose and stroked its fur at the same time and it said "*Boing-Boing!*"

Professor George was so startled he almost dropped the cat. He quickly tried again, rubbing the nose a little more gently and stroking the fur in a different place.

Once again the bionic cat said "*Boing-Boing.*"

He repeated this a third and fourth time. The result was still the same. The bionic cat always said "Boing-Boing."

"Oh no!" exclaimed Professor George. "I must have made a mistake when I **programmed** the voice section of the computer this morning. That's what happens when you try to do too much when you're tired and sleepy. You're sure to mess up somewhere."

"Oh well," he said with a big sigh. "I'll have to wait until I get home to fix it. I have to get to class now. There isn't enough time. Dan will just have to wait another day for his cat."

Chapter Four

Later that afternoon, Professor George was slowly walking home from the university, yawning at almost every step. It was hard to stay awake after working all night on the bionic cat.

Once again, he saw Daniel sitting on the front steps of his house. This time Daniel was looking worried. Professor George stopped and asked, "Dan, are you okay? Are you upset about not having a cat?"

"No," Daniel replied. "I wish it were. It's about my mum. She's sick in bed with the flu. The doctor says she has a temperature and is too ill to get up. He says that I have to be very quiet. I wish I had some way to cheer her up."

Professor George said, "I have something that will cheer up both of you. Come home with me and I'll show you."

Daniel smiled. Professor George always had surprises at his house. There were lots of tools and computer games. And best of all, it seemed, his wife always loved to make cookies.

Daniel was right. When they arrived she gave him a big chocolate cookie and a glass of milk.

"Come down to my workshop and see what's here," Professor George called from his basement.

Daniel jumped down the steps, three at a time. He looked around the room. He could hardly believe his eyes. In the middle of Professor George's worktable was a cat.

It did not look like any other cat, though. Its fur was very shiny. You could almost see through the fur.

But the cat was moving.

Daniel asked, "Is it a real cat, Professor George?"

"Well, it's sort of real," answered the Professor. "Here, I'll show you."

"See, it's a bionic cat," Professor George said as he showed Daniel how to turn it on with the switch under its tummy. "I built it from many of the electronic materials we use in my research lab, Dan."

Daniel could hardly believe his eyes when the bionic cat's eyes began to glow. "Hey, its tail is switching back and forth just like a real cat. And feel! It's starting to get warm," Daniel said.

"Wow! How does that happen?" Daniel asked.

"Well, when you said you wanted a real cat I thought that I should try and make it as real as possible. Cats are warm like you and me and so to make this one warm I have put in special low-power ceramic **heating** elements so that he can be at the same temperature as a real cat," answered Professor George.

"What else does it do?" asked Daniel.

"Put it on the floor and watch," replied the Professor.

Daniel put the bionic cat on the floor and looked up in surprise.

"Just look at it go!" exclaimed Daniel. "It walks like a real cat. You can hardly tell the difference.

"Wow!" shouted Daniel. "Look how it dodges right around the table legs.

"Hey, it doesn't run into the heater either! How does it know how to do all those things?" asked Daniel.

So, Professor George told him about the whiskers and the sensors. "These are very special types of ceramic materials, Dan. They are able to convert heat or

motion into electrical signals to control the cat. It is like the **nerves** in your fingers sending signals to your brain that something you touch is either hot or cold."

"So that is why it's a bionic cat," Daniel replied. "It has electronic controls that are like a real cat's biological controls."

"Great Dan," responded Professor George. "That is exactly right. You learn very quickly."

He then showed Daniel the little computer inside the bionic cat's tummy.

"It is very small so it does not use much energy, Dan," explained Professor George.

Next, Professor George said, "Here, you hold it and stroke its fur, Dan. But you must be very gentle because it is fibre-optic fur." He explained how the light travels down the fur and recharges the batteries when the cat sits in the sunlight.

Daniel was very gentle as he stroked the fur. "Listen!" he exclaimed. "Listen, it's purring. It's saying 'purrr, purrr, purrr,' just like a real cat. That is really fantastic! How does it do that?"

So Professor George showed Daniel the tiny little **voice box**, and told him all about programming the little computer to activate the voice box when the fur was stroked. Then he remembered.

"Oh no!" Professor George shouted in dismay. "I forgot all about the mistake I was going to fix before I showed you the bionic cat!"

Daniel asked, a little frightened, "What's wrong Professor George? Everything looks all right to me. The bionic cat is fantastic. What's the matter?"

Professor George answered, "Here, I'll show you Dan. This morning I was so sleepy that I made a mistake when I was programming the last part of the computer.

"Let your thumb rub the cat's nose at the same time as you stroke its fur and see what happens," said the Professor.

Daniel did as he was told and immediately the bionic cat said "Boing-Boing!"

Daniel laughed loudly. "It said 'Boing-Boing!' That's really funny. What's so bad about that, Professor George?"

Professor George answered, "It's supposed to say 'Meow-Meow, Meow-Meow.' All cats say 'Meow-Meow.' The computer will have to be reprogrammed to make it perfect."

Daniel replied, "But Professor George, this isn't just any old cat. This is a bionic cat. You just told me yourself a little while ago. It's perfectly okay for a bionic cat to say 'Boing-Boing' instead of 'Meow-Meow.' In fact, it seems just right for it to say 'Boing-Boing.' That makes it even more special."

"You mean you're not disappointed, Dan, because it says 'Boing-Boing'?"

Professor George asked.

"Of course not!" Daniel replied. "That makes the cat even better."

Professor George was surprised. He

thought that everything had to be perfect to be appreciated. Maybe he was wrong about that.

"You would like the cat just as it is?" Professor George asked Daniel.

"What? You mean it can be mine?"

shouted Daniel. "WOW! Can it?"

"Of course," replied the Professor. "I made it especially for you. Look at your arms. You have been holding it for awhile now. Do you see any red blotches? Have you been sneezing? Are your eyes watering?"

"Can I take it home to show Mum?" Daniel asked. "I'll bet it will cheer her up a lot."

"Of course you can," said Professor George, yawning. "What are you going to call it? Every cat has to have a name – even a bionic cat."

"Oh, that's easy," said Daniel. I'll call it 'Boing-Boing the Bionic Cat.' And every time it talks it will say its name, 'Boing-Boing'."

"That sounds good to me," said the professor, anxious to lie down for a nap.

Daniel ran home as fast as he could,

carrying Boing-Boing with him.

He was right – for as soon as he told his mother about Professor George and showed her the bionic cat and the wonderful things it could do, she began to feel better. And, when she rubbed the cat's nose and stroked its shiny fibre-optic fur and it said "Boing-Boing" she laughed and laughed. Then, Daniel knew she was going to be just fine.

THE END

Glossary

ALLERGY: A highly sensitive reaction of the body to substances like food or plant pollen or cat fur.

BATTERY: A portable device for storing and supplying electricity.

BIO: Indicates life or living organisms.

BIOENGINEERING: The design, development and use of materials and devices to help patients. Also to use engineering principles and methods to modify or produce biological products such as food.

BIONIC: Devices that combine electronic and biological features.

CERAMICS: Inorganic materials which are not metals. Examples include glass, pottery and bricks.

COMPUTER: An electronic machine which can be programmed to store information, solve problems and control machinery or electronic devices.

ELECTRICITY: A form of power or energy used for lighting, heating, working machinery or running computers.

ELECTRIC HEATER: A ceramic or metal heating element which gets hot when powered by electricity.

ELECTRONICS: Devices which can process, store and use electrical signals. Computers, TV sets, automatic washing machines operate with electronic devices.

ENGINEERING: The application of scientific principles to design, build and maintain mechanical, chemical or electrical devices or structures.

FIBRE OPTICS: Long, thin, flexible strands of glass or polymers that transmit light (photons) with very little loss of intensity. Used for communications and lighting.

GLASS: A hard, usually clear, material used for windows, light bulbs, storage containers and for drinking liquids.

MICROPROCESSOR: An electronic device that stores and manipulates information, such as numbers or words.

NERVES: Thread-like organ of the body which carries messages to and from the brain and other parts of the body, such as eyes, ears, heart, muscles, skin.

PIEZOELECTRIC CERAMICS: Special materials that generate electricity when squeezed or stretched. Conversely, materials that elongate or compress when a voltage is applied.

PROGRAM (COMPUTER): A set of instructions for a computer.

PUPILS (IN EYES): The small round opening in the middle of your eye, that looks black and which can grow larger to let more light in or get smaller to keep light out.

ROBOT: A machine, usually controlled by a computer or microprocessor, that acts like a living being, such as a human or a cat. (**Robotics** is the use of robots to perform tasks.)

SENSOR: A mechanical, chemical or electrical device that receives and responds to an external stimulus. Our eyes are sensors that respond to light. Our ears are sensors that respond to sound. Our tongue has sensors that respond to taste.

SOLAR CELL: An electronic device that converts the energy of sunlight (photons) into electrical energy.

SUPER COMPUTER: A computer that is able to store thousands of times more information and work thousands of times faster than a normal computer.

VOICE BOX: The part of the throat of a person or a cat that allows speaking, meowing, singing, roaring and other noises. Sometimes called the larynx.

VOICE SIMULATOR: An electronic voice that makes sounds controlled by a computer or microprocessor.

VOLTS: A unit of stored electrical potential.

IF THERE ARE OTHER WORDS in this Boing-Boing adventure that you do not know, write them here and look them up in a dictionary. Or write to Professor George at professor.george@boing-boing.org for a definition.

About the Author

Larry L. Hench, Ph.D., is currently Professor of Ceramic Materials at Imperial College, London and co-director of the Imperial College Tissue Engineering and Regenerative Medicine Centre. He also served as Professor of Material Science and Engineering for 32 years at The University of Florida. He is a member of the U.S. National Academy of Engineering.

A world-renowned scientist, graduate of The Ohio State University, and Fellow of The American Ceramic Society and the Royal Society of Chemistry – Hench's numerous achievements, honours, scholarly writings, and patents, over his 40 year career, span several fields; including: ceramics, glass and glass-ceramic materials, radiation damage, nuclear waste solidification, advanced optical materials, origins of life, ethics, technology transfer, bioceramics science and clinical applications.

He is credited with the discovery of Bioglass®, the first man-made material to bond to living bone – helping millions of people; and he continues to discover new applications in bioceramics for this amazing material.

His children's books extend his love of teaching, and science and engineering to a new generation. Everything built into the stories is scientifically valid and could be done. The inspiration for these books comes from his grandchildren.

Hench, an Ohio native, now divides his time between Hampshire, England and Florida in the United States. He and his wife, June Wilson, share four children and nine grandchildren.

About the illustrator

Ruth Denise Lear was born in Wilmslow, Cheshire, England in 1965, and lives now with her husband and three children in a rural village on the outskirts of Macclesfield, Cheshire.

Her love of drawing began in childhood and has never left her. She studied at Macclesfield College and has produced and sold paintings, cards, and etchings. Her favourite media are watercolour and ink, which have been used for the Boing-Boing series.

Boing-Boing the Bionic Cat is her first book, and she couldn't be more excited about it. Ruth says, "It is particularly apt that it should be about a cat, as I've always loved them very much-both wild and domestic; although I've never seen a bionic cat!" Not until now, anyway.

More information on both Larry and Ruth can be found on Boing-Boing's web site: www.boing-boing.org.

The Further Adventures of Boing-Boing

Boing-Boing the Bionic Cat and the Jewel Thief continues the adventures of Daniel, a young boy allergic to cats, and Boing-Boing the Bionic Cat, the amazing, robotic cat made for him by his kindly neighbour Professor George.

As a surprise for Daniel, Professor George adds a new ceramic part to the robotic cat he created, giving Boing-Boing the ability to "ROAR" like a lion! What Professor George doesn't realise is just how important this new feature will be.

What excitement awaits the invincible duo, Daniel and his bionic cat, during their trip to the natural history museum? Dinosaurs? Tigers? Whales? A Jewel Thief? During a Saturday afternoon trip to the museum, Daniel and Boing-Boing stumble into an adventure and soon learn that things aren't always as they seem.

Professor George, Boing-Boing, and Daniel bring engineering and science to life through the creation of a bionic cat and their exciting adventures and discoveries. This second book in the Boing-Boing the Bionic Cat series continues to entertain while teaching children about the evolving process of science, the benefits and limits of technology, and the caring and understanding from adult role models.

To read the first chapter of Boing-Boing's next adventure visit: www.boing-boing.org.

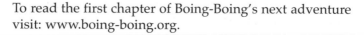

www.boing-boing.org

Find out more about Boing-Boing, Danny, Professor George and friends at Boing-Boing's web site.

Online you will find:
- Games
- Competitions
- Puzzles
- How to make your own bionic cat

And much, much more.

Kitty-Kits

Take a break, make a kit-kat.

Explore the world of robotic engineering with your very own Boing-Boing the Bionic Cat Kitty-Kits.

For more information visit Professor George's workshop at: www.boing-boing.org/workshop or follow the links from the home page.

Teachers and Schools

Boing-Boing is not just a house cat, you can find Boing-Boing in schools as well as part of a new cross-curriculum teaching scheme for seven year olds and up.

The objective of this scheme is to enhance the interest of primary school children, boys and girls, in the sciences, engineering and technology, and maintain that interest throughout their school years.

If you would like more information on this scheme, and to find out what teachers and schools think about Boing-Boing, please call the publisher or visit the Boing-Boing web site at: www.boing-boing.org.